D1452601

# Just What I Needed

# Also From Kylie Scott

*Famous In A Small Town*

*Pause*

*Fake*

*The Rich Boy*

*Lies*

*Repeat*

*It Seemed Like a Good Idea at the Time*

*Trust*

THE DIVE BAR SERIES
*Dirty*
*Twist*
*Chaser*

THE STAGE DIVE SERIES
*Lick*
*Play*
*Lead*
*Deep*
*Strong: A Stage Dive Novella*
*Love Song*
*The Rhythm Method*

THE FLESH SERIES
*Flesh*
*Skin*
*Flesh Series Novellas*

*Heart's a Mess*

*Colonist's Wife*

# Just What I Needed

A Stage Dive Novella
By Kylie Scott

1001 DARK NIGHTS
PRESS

Just What I Needed
A Stage Dive Novella
By Kylie Scott

Copyright 2022 Kylie Scott
ISBN: 979-8-88542-001-3

Foreword: Copyright 2014 M. J. Rose

Published by 1001 Dark Nights Press, an imprint of Evil Eye
Concepts, Incorporated

# Acknowledgments from the Author

A huge thank you to the 1,001 Dark Nights team. Working with you is always a pleasure. Your love and energy for the romance genre is a beautiful thing.

# One Thousand and One Dark Nights

*Once upon a time, in the future…*

*I was a student fascinated with stories and learning.
I studied philosophy, poetry, history, the occult, and
the art and science of love and magic. I had a vast
library at my father's home and collected thousands
of volumes of fantastic tales.*

*I learned all about ancient races and bygone
times. About myths and legends and dreams of all
people through the millennium. And the more I read
the stronger my imagination grew until I discovered
that I was able to travel into the stories… to actually
become part of them.*

*I wish I could say that I listened to my teacher
and respected my gift, as I ought to have. If I had, I
would not be telling you this tale now.
But I was foolhardy and confused, showing off
with bravery.*

*One afternoon, curious about the myth of the
Arabian Nights, I traveled back to ancient Persia to
see for myself if it was true that every day Shahryar
(Persian: شهريار, "king") married a new virgin, and then
sent yesterday's wife to be beheaded. It was written
and I had read that by the time he met Scheherazade,
the vizier's daughter, he'd killed one thousand
women.*

*Something went wrong with my efforts. I arrived in the midst of the story and somehow exchanged places with Scheherazade — a phenomena that had never occurred before and that still to this day, I cannot explain.*

*Now I am trapped in that ancient past. I have taken on Scheherazade's life and the only way I can protect myself and stay alive is to do what she did to protect herself and stay alive.*

*Every night the King calls for me and listens as I spin tales. And when the evening ends and dawn breaks, I stop at a point that leaves him breathless and yearning for more. And so the King spares my life for one more day, so that he might hear the rest of my dark tale.*

*As soon as I finish a story... I begin a new one... like the one that you, dear reader, have before you now.*

# Chapter One

There are reasons why people with careers like mine don't tend to date. Most notably, when the hell would we find the time and energy?

I regularly chase after a small child up to six days a week. It depends on what's going on with the family. My day usually starts at eight despite Jameson waking at around six or so. And it finishes at different hours depending on what's happening. Some celebrity parents want a nanny to be available twenty-four seven. Some would even basically like you to raise the child in question.

Once, for instance, I was offered a job living in an apartment with two children under the age of two while the parents occupied a mansion nearby. Their plan was to drop by once a day, time permitting, to visit with their kids.

I declined that one.

But the people I work for currently, David Ferris (from the world-famous rock band Stage Dive) and his wife Evelyn, are more hands-on. Which is great. And more importantly, they enjoy waking with their son, allowing me to keep my sacred morning rituals intact.

The truth is, I don't want to start work any earlier than eight. I hate having to fake being a morning person. It's rude and wrong and shouldn't be allowed. Both my faith in humanity and ability to get things done is vastly improved after two coffees and a long, hot shower. With emphasis on the words long and hot. The move from L.A. to Portland has been great. I enjoy being back in my hometown. What I do not love, however, is the weather. And November in Oregon is colder than I remember. Guess I got soft down in California. But the coldness—and the constant chasing after a toddler—has seemed to contribute to my sex life.

Or rather, lack thereof.

Which is why it's surprising on several levels to find a half-naked male in the guest house's kitchen first thing in the morning. I myself am dressed in my usual sensible oversized plaid pajamas and fluffy socks. He, however, is wearing a pair of those thin, soft cotton sleep pants and nothing else. Not a damn thing. And let me tell you, those pants are sitting dangerously low on his hips. Though the real kicker is the dusting of dark hair leading down from his belly button to the bulge beneath his thin cotton of his sleep pants. I cannot look away. It's impossible.

"Hi," he says cheerfully.

Like I said, due to time restraints, it's been a while since I've gotten laid. And this half-naked man is a lot to deal with this early in the day. It feels like it takes approximately an hour for my sleep-stunned gaze to travel upwards. From his crotch to his abs, then his pecs, thick muscular neck, and finally his handsome bemused face. All while he stands there with a cup of coffee in hand smirking at me. Oh, the shame.

"I'm Dean," he says. "The record producer."

"R-right," I stutter. And try to punch through the cloudiness of my sleepy brain to make sense of his words.

"And I'm guessing you're Jude the nanny?"

"Yes." He knows my name, which means he might have a reason to be in my kitchen. But I'm having a hard time forming coherent thought, between my need for caffeine and the distraction of his cover model good looks.

He threads his fingers through his longish dark hair and

asks, "Do you need coffee?"

"I really do."

"Let me get out of your way then." He wanders over to the dining table and takes a seat. "Sorry I arrived so late last night. I hope I didn't wake you."

"No. You're, um…no." And it all starts to come back to me. Dave and Ev mentioned that a work friend was coming to town and asked if it was okay if he stayed here in the guest house with me. What they didn't mention is that he's one of the hottest men in existence.

"Good," he says with another smile. As if I am the most amusing woman in the world.

Yay me.

His gaze takes me in from my messy blonde bedhead to my fluffy red socks. No doubt he is wishing he was as warm and comfortable as me instead of flaunting himself like a hussy. Or the thought might not even cross his mind, which would also be fine and dandy given how much I'm enjoying the view.

The guest house is similar in style to the main house. It's beautiful and roomy and made of wood with a gray stone fireplace feature. Lots of tall glass windows to let in the light. And of course, the weak morning light loves him. Casting all of the ridges and planes of his body in seductive shadows.

But back to the details about the guest house.

There are two bedrooms, each with their own bathroom, and a deck to sit out on in the summer. This is the first time I've shared the space since moving in upon its completion a couple of months ago. Not having a roommate was nice. Having the option of staring at this man, however, is…wow. My hormones are bestirred for what feels like the first time in forever. Which is a little embarrassing.

I fill the largest mug I can find with the perfect mixture of coffee and creamer.

*Come to me, caffeine. Fill me with joy and turn on my brain. Pretty please.*

Now that I'm partially awake, I can see small signs of cohabitation. Like the acoustic guitar sitting on the sofa. There's something romantic and soulful about a man who is a musician. Not even spending time around Stage Dive's manic drummer, Malcolm Ericson, has cured me entirely of those teenage dreams.

Dean is still sitting at the table with a faint smile on his face watching me when I turn around and start working on breakfast. Sheesh. This level of scrutiny when I'm still waking up is intense.

"You're a morning person, aren't you?" I ask, waiting for the toaster to pop.

He lifts one brazenly bare shoulder in a half shrug. The temerity of the man. "Probably more of a night person. It comes with the work. Musicians don't usually tend to be early risers. But since all of the Stage Dive guys have families to get back to…"

I put the Pop-Tarts on two plates and take them over to the table. "Breakfast is served."

"Thank you." He has a disarmingly cute smile. "I appreciate that."

And I say nothing. No way is he hot and nice. Those two qualities never exist in the same person. Impossible.

This is the problem with not having a social or sexual life. You lose your touch. Those muscles wither and die from disuse. You forget how to do it—how to talk to people. Most of my discussions with nine-month-old Jamesy involve making airplane or farm animal noises while coaxing him to eat his vegetables. Which leaves me standing there hesitating with a Pop-Tart in one hand and a coffee in the other and no social skills at all. Not a single clue what to say to start a normal adult conversation. I am hopelessly screwed when it comes to dealing with someone like him. Every time I look at him, my brain turns into a consistency similar to the baby's food. Just mush. A normal person would take the opportunity to get to know this alarmingly attractive guy who I will be cohabitating with for the foreseeable future. But I can't bring myself to do it. *Shit.*

"Um," I say like a genius. "Have a nice day."

\* \* \* \*

There are definite perks to my job. I often get to travel and stay in nice hotels. And there's usually time for me to do a little sightseeing. I worked for a couple of different families down in L.A. before returning to the Pacific Northwest. I was with a famous acting duo and their children for several years. And before that a diva with a toddler. Now *that* household was wild. It was hard to judge who was more emotionally mature somedays. But once you're ducking objects thrown by both the adult and the child, it's time to get out. The Ferris family and their friends have been kind to me. It makes for a great low-stress situation. Usually.

"I declare this recording studio open for business," says Evelyn Ferris, holding a bottle of champagne aloft as she presents the new building to all of us standing around outside. "I'm not really supposed to break this, am I? Isn't that just for ships?"

Lena Ferris lines up another shot with her high-tech camera. "I say we drink it instead."

"That's a much better idea." Ev lowers the bottle.

Jimmy and Ben are already busy inside the new studio (which no doubt cost a small fortune to build) located to one side of the property. But Mal and David are present and clapping politely. Okay. So Mal is actually twirling a drumstick while making loud hooting noises. But honestly, for him, that's pretty normal behavior and to be expected. From what I've seen, he's a little like a toddler. It's when they go quiet that you should be ready for chaos.

The band's producer and my new housemate, Dean

Jennings, is also present. This is evident in the way every fine hair on my body is standing at attention. He's fully dressed this time, but it doesn't matter. You would think hiding all of the tanned skin and muscles would diminish the overall effect of the man. My knees, however, are as weak as can be. I have observed over time that the usual musician's attire is jeans, sneakers or boots, and a worn tee advertising some band you've probably never heard of. Given the time of year, there's now often also a hoodie included. And he wears it *damn* well.

I need to know if this man has any negatives. Because from outward appearances, he's too good to be true. I bet he leaves dirty clothes on the floor and wet towels on the bed and hogs the covers on a cold winter's night. He probably has all of those annoying habits and more. Thereby making him more fallible. Meaning I will definitely be less likely to get all up in my feelings each time I see him. Because this level of awkward and lusting isn't sustainable. Not for me. And you just know the prime feeling I am presently experiencing is coming from the pants region. If someone could invent a switch to specifically to turn off your libido, I sure would appreciate it.

Please and thank you.

"We meet again," he says with a smile that seems a touch more than just friendly.

"Yeah." Just like the last time, I'm at a loss for words around him.

His eyes are this beautiful dreamy pale green color. I don't think I noticed them earlier. But I have never seen anything like them. They're so pretty. His lashes are long and dark, and there are faint sunlines radiating from the corners like he spends a lot of time outside or something. I would guess he's in his early thirties. A little older than my twenty-five, which is not necessarily a problem. Though there's every chance he's going to think me gauche and girlish with the way I'm acting.

*Ugh. No. Enough of the internal negative talk.*

What is an issue, however, is the way I have still only managed to say one damn word to the man.

"Hey, Dean."

He still doesn't say anything else. He just smiles his smile. It's definitely a different one than the polite, professional smile he gave the others. At least, I think it is. It seems to suggest he finds me of interest for some reason. Or at a minimum, that I amuse him.

This would be so much easier if I could just read his mind and find out if he's interested. And you can bet that the sight of this particular smile makes my stomach swoop and my blood run hot. I have got it bad for this boy.

Here, once again, is where a normal person would take the opportunity to do something. To flirt or express an interest in the man or just plain strike up a conversation…I don't know. But no, I stand there in silence like an idiot with the baby monitor clutched in my hands in case my charge wakes early from his afternoon nap. I used to have confidence. No idea where I left it. I hope he doesn't notice the spot of pumpkin smeared on my blue jeans. Dean. Not Jamesy. The baby is, after all, the one who put it there.

"I better get back to it," he says finally, giving me a chin tip. "See you later, Jude."

"Bye." Another whole word. I am a legend.

He heads back into the recording studio as I stand there and watch him go. Like a loser. Which is when I realize that I am also being watched. Mal is still busy twirling his drumsticks. But the rest of the group are giving me distinctly curious glances. Like I have all of their attention.

"Is everything okay?" I ask.

"Sure," says David. "Right, baby?"

Ev's smile seems off somehow. "Absolutely."

David then gives me a broad smile and two thumbs up. Which is weird. He has always been professional and friendly.

But this is…I don't actually know what this is, to be honest.

Mal, meanwhile, throws a drumstick in the air like a baton and catches it. He then gives himself an enthusiastic round of applause. There's a person who definitely has no issues with making himself heard. I need a little of his confidence. Especially seeing as he has enough for at least eight people.

He and David head back into the recording studio.

"Time to get out of the cold and drink champagne," says Lena, heading for the house.

The three of us womenfolk follow the stone path through the garden. Not that there's much happening at this time of year. The property is on the edge of a hill overlooking Mount Hood. It's a beautiful view. Though the wind is chill and bitter as heck.

"Are you getting along okay with Dean?" asks Ev. "You'd tell me if you felt uncomfortable sharing the guest house with him, right?"

"Of course," I say. "But we're fine so far. He seems nice."

"He is a really nice guy."

"And hot," adds Lena. "Don't you think, Jude?"

Oh my God. My laughter is powered by pure nervous energy. It splutters up and out of me before I can smack a hand over my mouth to stop it. Cringe.

Lena grins. As if that is all the encouragement she needs to pursue this line of questioning. Not good.

It's a relief to get back into the warm air of the main house. Ev heads for the bar and sets out three champagne flutes. And since she's the boss, I will of course do as told and have a sip or two. Celebrities always have the best booze and such. You'd be amazed how much free stuff some of them get sent. The section of the population who actually have the disposable income to afford all of the nice things don't often need to spend the money to get them.

Gold and platinum records line the hallway, and guitars are scattered around everywhere. When I started, I worked as both housekeeper and nanny for the family. But then they moved from their apartment in the Pearl District to this much larger place, so they got a full-time housekeeper to cook and clean. A good thing since this place is huge. It also means I can just focus on keeping up with Jamesy. With the way he's attempting to get into everything these days, he is more than enough for me.

"Dean's single too," says Lena, getting comfortable on the sofa. "In case you're interested. He was seeing a swimsuit model. What was her name? It starts with G. Gabby or Greta or Gianna…something like that."

Ev frowns. "Don't let his ex intimidate you, though, Jude."

"Absolutely not," says Lena. "You're a wonderful woman with a great personality. And not all of us can have the kind of booty that appears on the cover of magazines."

"Right." My smile won't stick to my face for some reason. It's been a long time since I last pondered the state of my booty. "Thanks."

"You're not seeing anyone, are you, Jude?" asks Evelyn. "You haven't mentioned anyone. Not that you're required to tell us your private business, of course."

"Um. No."

Lena grins. "I think you and Dean would make a cute couple. Don't you think he's handsome?"

I nod helplessly. Because the man is handsome as fuck. And this is all so awkward. I smooth down my blonde bangs and say a whole lot of nothing. It's becoming a habit of late.

"I repeat, not that we're sticking our noses into your personal life because that would be wrong," says Ev, passing me a glass of champagne.

"Totally wrong," Lena agrees.

"So very wrong. Yes."

"Anyway, Dean's been super successful the last few years," says Lena, still going full steam ahead. "All of the biggies want him onboard as their producer. Ever since he got nominated for a Grammy, he's been the one to work with."

Ev nods. "That's true."

"So…" Lena crosses her legs and asks, "What do you think, Jude?"

Now this situation is humiliating on several levels.

Let me explain.

Not only are we talking about the viability of a man who is hopelessly out of my league. But, to my great shame, when I started this job, I had a small crush on Jimmy Ferris. Yes, Lena's husband. I know, I know. There is no excuse for crushing on a married man. It is a terrible and tacky thing to do. Though meeting the person who used to feature predominantly on the posters covering your teenage bedroom walls is an experience. But I totally have it under control now and hardly ever blush brighter than a baboon's butt in his presence. Like it's a fifty-fifty thing. A vast improvement, really. Those early days were awkward as hell.

The other issue is that I would very much prefer it if these rich, famous, and cool people didn't know what a pathetic figure I am. A twenty-five-year-old with no social life who hasn't dated since dinosaurs roamed the earth. My favorite of which by the way is the diplodocus. I've started reading dinosaur books to Jamesy recently. He likes it when I make roaring noises.

And there I go proving my own point.

Again.

I have no life.

"You okay?" asks Ev with a gentle smile. "You're not saying much."

"Ah…"

Lena's brows arch high on her face. "Oh no. Did we go too far? Have we scared you off?"

These women are so kind and supportive. The way they're now nervously exchanging glances as if they might have upset me somehow. I can't do it. I can't lie to them. They are, after all, the closest thing I have to actual friends right now. And the truth is, I could do with some friends.

My mouth opens, and it all spills out. "He was standing in the kitchen half dressed this morning, and my eyes nearly fell out of my head. I mean, I had absolutely no cool. I almost choked on my own tongue. The man is a health hazard. He is without a doubt the most attractive male I have ever seen in my existence. But more than that, he seems so nice. And I don't know what to say. I just don't. I honestly haven't been this inept when it comes to the opposite sex since middle school. It's like it's been so long since my hormones actually woke up and took notice of someone, I've forgotten how all of that works." I pause to take a breath, and then cringe. "I don't know how to date. Hell. I don't even remember how to flirt. He talks to me, and my brain blanks. I just stand there like a complete idiot. It's a total disaster!"

By the end of my speech, Lena's brows are just about lost in her hairline they're so high. Ev, meanwhile, seems to have frozen in place.

*Shit.* "I, um–"

"Stop. That was a lot, but it's okay," says my boss before pausing to take a sip of champagne. "Don't worry, Jude. We've got you. We're going to help you win over Dean."

Lena claps her hands excitedly. "This is going to be so much fun."

# Chapter Two

"I'm not so sure about this," I say. Though I doubt anyone heard me from beneath the layers of the deep conditioning treatment on my hair and sheet mask on my face. They were also pretty busy selecting outfits for me from the range of clothes and accessories Anne bought over. She, like me, has booty but not much breast. When she isn't heavily pregnant with her second child as she is currently, of course.

"A makeover is always a worthwhile investment in time and resources," answers Lena. "Trust us, Jude. Good hair and makeup paired with a great outfit can give your confidence a huge boost."

Ev holds up a red halter neck gown. "This is seriously sexy."

"Yeah, but what possible excuse can she make for hanging out at home in an evening gown?" Anne, the voice of reason, sits on the floor pushing a wooden toy train around for Jamesy. He's adorable and delighted by all of the attention. Having someone to play with is basically peak happiness for a small child. It's right up there with cuddles and cake.

"I haven't shaved my legs in a while, either," I say.

Anne nods somberly. "I can't even reach mine. I assume they're still there, but with this bump, seeing anything below my belly button is an issue."

"Leg hair is not a problem. We can work with that." Ev moves on to a pair of leather leggings. "These are very cool girl rock star. I say they have possibilities."

"And they're wipe clean," says Anne. "Much more practical than you'd imagine. Just don't be foolish like me and attempt to wear them in warm weather. Leather does not breathe."

My own wardrobe was quickly deemed insufficient for the mission of winning me a man. A decision that was harsh but fair. Being a nanny is usually more about comfort and convenience than style. I have a fine selection of tees, sweaters, jeans, and leggings. My current position doesn't really have a dress code. Not a bad thing. One job I heard of required you to wear baggy, boring clothing in the hope that the man of the house wouldn't turn his wandering eye your way. I mean, it's not like affairs between celebrities and nannies never happen. Google the topic. The rumors are rife. But that seemed a bit extreme to me.

Another contract I was offered detailed the need to fit in with both the child and their parents' chosen aesthetic by wearing certain brands in specific colors when out in public. Which would be fine if the position included a clothing allowance. Which it did not. Some rich people are super demanding while being cheap.

"Maybe this was a bad idea," I say, feeling the tiniest bit overwhelmed by just about everything.

"Don't say that." Ev adds a black cashmere vest to the keep pile. "A defeatist attitude will not be tolerated. Dean is great, and you want him, and we are going to help you get him. End of story."

"Have you guys told her about you know what?" Anne tickles the baby's bare foot. Jamesy waves his sock in the air and laughs his little heart out. There is nothing as pure and sweet as the sound of a baby laughing.

Meanwhile, Lena and Ev exchange glances, which isn't weird or worrying at all.

"Told me about what?" I ask.

"It's not a big deal," says Ev. "I mean, it happened years ago."

I say nothing and wait.

Lena grimaces and says, "I may have momentarily dated Dean. It was only for like five minutes, just before Jimmy and I got together."

"Oh," I say.

Here's the thing, Lena Ferris is kind of gorgeous. Curvy with dark hair and wit and style for days. And I...I'm me. An expert at making faces to distract crying children. A veritable ninja when it comes to swaddling infants. And I dare anyone to outdo me in the task of persuading small, cranky children to get dressed. Once upon a time, I had outside interests. But that was a while back now. This whole dating idea is a disaster. Maybe I'm just not meant to be in a relationship. After all, what would Dean and I even talk about?

"This is not a negative," says Ev. "It just means he has good taste in women and that we have some inside knowledge. Such as..."

Lena sits up straight. "We know he is not a dick to the women he dates."

"A very good thing."

Out of nowhere, Jamesy unleashes a noise best described as a yodel. So I do the polite thing and yodel back, earning myself a smile consisting of two small teeth and a truly remarkable amount of spit. Babies are such an even mixture of cute and gross.

"We should go over proposed topics of discussion," says Evelyn. "You could ask him about his work and life. Draw him out like that."

Lena continues sorting through the pile of clothes. "Most men do enjoy being the center of attention."

"There will always be time to tell him about yourself later."

Anne cocks her head. "Wait a minute. Which of you two wound up in a relationship because you pandered to the dude in question?"

"These are just some tips to see her through the start," says Ev.

"Until she feels more comfortable," agrees Lena.

Anne narrows her gaze on the two women. "Evelyn, the night you met David, you threw up multiple times. Including on him, from what I've heard. And Lena, I distinctly remember you telling Jimmy off the night I first met you."

Ev sighs. "Why do people always talk about the puking?"

"To be fair," says Lena, "those were both quite different and complicated situations."

"But you were both being your own sweet selves. That's the point I'm trying to make here." Anne looks at her watch. "You can lose the face mask, Jude. Just out of interest, did they actually ask your permission before turning you into their own personal experimental dating Barbie doll?"

"Anne, you're so salty," says Lena with a raised brow. "This is quite unlike you."

"Deal with it. My mood has been set to awful for days. Though that doesn't mean I don't also have a valid point." Her shoulders sag tiredly. "Let's just say I am having serious second thoughts about birthing a another child. Especially since said child is constantly pushing on my bladder and kicking all night, keeping me awake. Thank goodness this baby is due to get the heck out of me in four weeks."

"To answer your question, it's fine. I really do need the help." I carefully peel the face mask thing off and pat my face dry with a hand towel. "All right, what's next?"

At that, Lena's eyes light up. "Now it's time for your hair and makeup."

\* \* \* \*

When Dean walks in the door at around eight, I'm ready. i.e. Primped to within an inch of my life with my hair in a slick ponytail and a natural-looking full face of makeup. I'm not going to lie, the high-heeled booties took some work. It's been a while since I wore four-inch heels. To be honest, I don't know that I've ever actually worn four-inch heels. I tend to top out at three. But the girls did a great job putting an outfit together for me. The leather leggings and white silk shirt look sublime. Nothing like how I usually dress, but impressive just the same. And what does reality have to do with impressing someone anyway? Nothing. That's what. While anxiety continues to have me in its cold and clammy grip, I refuse to let it stop me.

"Hey," he says, his eyes going wide. "You look nice."

"Thanks."

"Are you heading out?"

"No. I thought, I just…I was in the mood." He waits for me to say more. But that's all I have in me. "Yeah."

"Okay."

He moves on to pulling off his hoodie, accidentally lifting the bottom of his tee in the process. Such a nice slice of tanned skin and stomach. It's good to know his body has lost none of the allure of this morning. The proof being that my loins are wide awake and giving him their full attention. He really is something. Then he smiles again and just looks at me. Like he's waiting for me to make my next move. Considering how limited my moves are, this could be over quickly.

"Are you hungry?" I ask.

"I could definitely eat," he chuckles.

"Great. That's great." I feel like I'm going to start fidgeting at any moment, so it's probably best to begin the meal part of the plan.

Lena and Ev initially had plans for a three-course candlelit dinner. They even discussed hiring a violinist at one stage. But

Anne wisely suggested keeping things low-key. Thank goodness. Best not to spook the poor man by springing a surprise formal date on him. Or put more pressure on me. Though I did light a couple of pillar candles because I like candles. I find their gentle light soothing after a long day.

I pull the platter of sushi out of the fridge and nod to the sofa. Glasses, napkins, plates, and a bottle of sake sit waiting on the coffee table. "We might as well be comfortable."

"You've gone to some effort," he says as he walks over to the sofa.

"Consider this your welcome dinner." I follow and pour him a glass of sake.

"Okay. Thanks," he takes it and starts to look a bit intense, which makes me more nervous.

"But don't let it go to your head," I blurt out. "Pop-Tarts are still on the menu for breakfast."

Look at me go. Another whole sentence. This is where my practiced lines run out, however, and I have to start winging it. Yikes.

"I'll look forward to it," he takes a sip and then gives me a slow smile.

Holy shit. His smile and the way it lights his gaze makes me giddy. Like my heart is filled with heat and my rib cage has grown wings or something. I need to calm down and do some deep breathing. This is not love at first sight. It is like at first coffee. But it's been a while since I felt anything similar. Hence my brain going into meltdown and my hormones running wild. Despite all of these distractions, I manage to carry the platter to the living room without tripping in the high heels. I would high-five myself if he wasn't watching. We sit on the sofa and pick up the chopsticks. This is it. Our first ever meal together. Fingers crossed it isn't our last.

"It was good of you to organize this," he says. "Sushi is a favorite of mine."

"Lena said you liked it."

His brows draw down slightly. "She did, huh?"

"Yeah." Not sure if mentioning her name is a good idea or not. But it's done now. We focus on eating for a minute. My hands are only shaking a little from nerves. Perhaps I can pull this off after all. The girls suggested asking him lots of questions about himself. That I can do. "How did your first day in the studio go?"

"Good. I've worked with the guys a couple of times over the years. It's nice to finally get to be the producer steering the process. What with them being one of my favorite bands and all," he says. "Are you a music fan?"

"I played flute in my middle school band."

"Flute is cool."

"Lizzo has done a lot for positive flute representation in the media lately."

He laughs. "She sure has."

"But I like listening to music too."

"What are some of your favorites?"

And that's when it happens. My mouth is open and waiting. My chopsticks are tensed. And the salmon sashimi topped with pickled ginger, wasabi, and a dash of soy sauce somehow slips and goes into freefall. Though it doesn't just fall, it slides down the front of my white silk shirt. Or Anne's designer white silk shirt, as the case may be. This cool put-together version of me didn't even last five minutes in the real world.

I could almost cry. Seriously.

Dean passes me a wad of napkins. Not that there's anything to be done. Leather pants might be wipe clean, but the rest is going to take some work.

"What can I do to help?" he asks.

"The shirt isn't even mine. It probably cost a fortune," I moan and collect the remains of the sashimi from the polished wooden floor. "Can you look up how to get soy sauce stains out of silk, please?"

He pulls his cell out of his back jeans pocket and gets busy. "Here we go. It says to soak it in lukewarm water and a little washing liquid."

I nod and start in on the buttons on my way to the laundry. A bucket is filled with water and the washing liquid added. Hopefully getting it treated quickly helps. My mind is one hundred percent on the silk shirt. It doesn't even occur to me that I am now walking around half naked until I walk back out into the living area. Dean freezes like a deer in headlights at the sight of my beige lace bra. The nicest underwear I own. It is sort of sheer and definitely pricey. He looks at me, and I look at him, and neither of us do anything for the longest moment.

What breaks the thrall is the woman banging on the glass door leading onto the deck. Wow is she glaring at us. There is actual fire in her eyes. Her face is also horribly familiar. Like home page of online magazines familiar. Long, dark hair and a shapely body.

I cross my arms over my chest to cover the essentials. Not that she couldn't see even less on a beach.

"Frankie?" asks Dean, his mouth hanging open just a little. "What are you doing here?"

"Freezing my ass off." The woman outside huffs and puffs, her breath steaming the cold air. "Can you let me in, please?"

Behind her stands Ziggy, one of the security guards. Both of his hands are taken up with the woman's designer luggage. Guess Lena was wrong about Dean's ex-girlfriend's name starting with G. Though F is close. Frankie Manning is a real live actual supermodel. And I had the nerve to try to romance her ex. Mind you, if they are exes, it would be nice to know exactly why she is here.

Before opening the door, Dean passes me the hoodie he discarded earlier, which I appreciate, and gives me an unreadable look.

Frankie stomps inside in her own four-inch heel booties, throwing her sheepskin jacket on the couch and pausing to pop a piece of sushi into her mouth. Unlike me, she is at home in the heels and makeup and everything. She makes it work. "You're never going to believe this. I had a shoot booked with Richard on the coast, and I told him not to hire me if he was hiring Molly. The bitch had the audacity to take a swing at me last time we had to work together, and that is not okay. She needs help from a professional. But I turn up and guess who's there?"

Ziggy deposits the bags inside the door, nods, and disappears back out into the night.

"Molly?" asks Dean.

"It's like you said. Not only is his name Dick, but he is soul deep committed to being one." Frankie turns to me with a curious gaze. "Who is this?"

"This is my new friend Jude."

"I'm so sorry for disturbing your date," she says, stealing another piece of sushi off the platter. The way she pops it between her lush lips without disturbing her lip gloss is real talent.

I cross my arms over my chest once again, despite the hoodie. "Oh, it's not a date. We were, um, we were just having dinner."

Dean gives me a glance. No idea what it means.

"Not a date, huh?" asks Frankie, finishing chewing and focusing her full attention on Dean. "Because, hon, I was hoping we could talk. I've been rethinking some things lately. If we could talk in private? If you don't mind, Jude?"

"Frankie," says Dean with a frown. "This isn't right. You can't just barge in here and take over."

"Don't give me that look, hon. It won't take long, I promise."

Okay. I can read his look this time. It's an apologetic one. "It's fine," I say, heading for my bedroom. "Nice to meet you."

"You're so sweet, Jude!" Frankie gives me a finger wave. "See you later."

Now Dean is shoving a hand through his dark hair. If anything, he seems frustrated. But he doesn't say another word.

As soon as I get behind my closed bedroom door, I slump dramatically. Then I get the torture booties off my feet. My poor innocent toes. Now it would be a lie to say I am not disappointed. But there's no way I'm going to compete for the man's affections with a freaking supermodel. Not a chance. They're obviously still close and talk often. Maybe they were just on a break. It happens. Or maybe they have an open relationship. Whatever. It's none of my business.

I take a selfie before beginning the process of removing all of my makeup. Because Lena did a great job. I look amazing. There's every chance I needed reminding of this fact, how I can dress up and have a life outside of my job. Of course, my heart and groin are sad about Dean. It's amazing how quickly you can get carried away and start imagining happy ever afters. Especially with the help of hormones. But oh well. I can choose to see the positive side of this experience and view it as a wakeup call. Might be time for me to make some effort and contact a few old friends. See if they want to go out Saturday night.

I give my reflection a pleased nod.

It's a plan.

# Chapter Three

My empty stomach wakes me at around one in the morning. Because I definitely did not go back out there again after being sent to my room by Frankie. Not that that's what she did exactly. Some people just have big personalities. Or maybe I am a little jealous and cranky because she got the man. It's only been a day since we met. I'm sure I'll get over the disappointment soon. Anyway. I creep out to the kitchen. Odds are Dean and his guest are in the throes of a heated reunion. But the house is quiet. Maybe they've already done their sexing and settled down to sleep for the night.

A cold wind is blowing a gale outside, but we're safe and warm within. By the fridge light, I inspect my snacking options. There's no sushi left, naturally. But there are the other necessary basics in life. Some slices of cheese, turkey, and pickles. With a couple of Oreos for after, of course.

"Hey," says a deep voice from out of the dark.

I jump and hug the jar of pickles to me like their poor innocent green lives depend on it. Which they do. "Holy shit."

"Sorry." He ruffles a hand through his mussed hair. And once again, he's half naked. This is outrageous, all of this male nipple showing. The man should be ashamed of his beautiful body. And I should not be repeating the crime of lusting after someone who is taken. What a seriously bad idea. "Didn't mean to scare you, Jude."

"Where did you come from?"

"I was just sleeping on the couch."

My mouth opens, but nothing comes out. Finally, I manage a whispered, "You were?"

"Yeah. Got hungry, huh?" he asks, leaning his hip against the kitchen counter. "I wanted to apologize for earlier. For Frankie just showing up like that. She, ah…she's kind of hard to predict. She tends to make her own rules. But I'm sorry our dinner got interrupted."

"That's fine." I put the jar of pickles on the counter. "It's no big deal."

"It wasn't?"

I just shrug. Which is about when I realize I'm still wearing his hoodie. It was just so cozy and smelled like him, so I decided to allow myself that one little treat.

Dammit. I had totally forgotten.

Talk about busted.

There was definite sniffing of the item of clothing earlier. I got high off the scent of his cologne, and I am only mildly ashamed. It would be great, however, if I could stop embarrassing myself by doing these sorts of things. My luck with men and ability to be cool are on the same low level these days. "I, ah, was cold. Let me give you this back."

"No rush."

But rush is exactly what I do. I tear the item of clothing off over my head, where it of course gets caught on my ponytail. Dignity and poise are for other people. It might explain why I spend so much of my time hanging out with toddlers. They do tend to be simpler and more straightforward than most adults. They also are not the least bit cool or have a clue about social cues and manners. They make choosing chaos a valid lifestyle choice.

When I finally emerge, he's standing there giving me a smile. The same smile that befuddled me for the better part of yesterday. It would be nice to say I am now immune, but alas. Beneath his hoodie, I'm wearing a white tank and pajama pants, and not much else. It would be so great if my nipples could not be hard. I would really appreciate that a lot.

I hand the sweatshirt over. "Here you go."

"Thanks." He gives me a long look. "Jude, you mind if I ask you a question?"

"Sure."

"Something Frankie said got me thinking. Were we on a date earlier?"

"Oh," I say with much wisdom. "That."

"It's just that you were all dressed up and ordered in sushi and it felt like maybe it was meant to be something special. Something more than just two people sharing a dinner and getting to know each other."

My mouth opens, but nothing comes out. Nada. Not a word.

And he just waits.

I haven't given it a great deal of thought. But I think it probably would be easier to talk to the man if he was wearing more clothes. There is, however, no polite way of telling him to cover his man chest. Not in a way that wouldn't lead him to believe I have issues regarding the ogling of said man chest. Because keeping my gaze on his face is a chore. Though the light from the fridge casts his cheekbones and jawline in the most interesting shadows. He is a work of art. Honestly.

I wince. "You're just going to stand there silently until I answer, aren't you?"

He nods.

"Great," I mumble. Then I squeeze my eyelids shut tight, take a deep breath, and open them once again. "Okay. Here's the problem with me giving you an honest answer, Dean. This is embarrassing. We only met not quite twenty-four hours ago. We don't know each other. And your supermodel girlfriend showed up and I assume wanted to talk to you about the chances of getting back together. That is why she asked to talk to you in private, right?"

He hesitates but then nods again.

"Right," I mutter.

The way the line of his muscular neck moves as he swallows shouldn't be so sexy. "Frankie and I aren't getting back together. We want different things. We've tried being together a couple of times now, and we work as friends, but that's all."

"Okay."

He takes a small step forward and speaks softly. "You going to answer the question for me now?"

"I'd really honestly rather not," I say and drop my gaze to the floor. "It's kind of embarrassing."

"I kind of need you to."

"Need is a strong word." I glance up.

"I feel it's accurate in this case." One side of his lips rise. "Please, Jude?"

*Ugh.* "Yes," I finally admit. "You would not be wrong if you took my actions as being somewhat date-like."

He takes a step closer. "You usually spring surprise dates on people?"

"No. I'm sorry. I haven't actually been on one in forever. It's why I'm so bad at all of this. But…"

"But?"

"Nothing." I sigh. "I answered your question. My middle of the night snack is waiting. Are we done here?"

"No." He takes another step closer, trapping me between his body and the kitchen counter. "Not yet. The thing is, I am fine with you springing surprise dates on me. Just so you know."

"You are?" I breathe out the words.

"I am." His voice is deep. Strong.

My heart beats double-time. "That's really nice to hear."

"That's the other reason why Frankie and I aren't going to be trying again. Because I like you. Getting involved with her again wouldn't be right when she's not the girl I've got on my mind." He smiles. "I know we just met, but I want to know more about you."

My eyes feel as wide as twin moons. "You do?"

"Though this situation is a little complicated. We're both stuck here with work for the foreseeable future. If things don't work out between us…"

"Right. That's, um, a valid point."

"Do you still want to see where this goes?"

I think it over. "It is a concern. I agree with you there. But I think we're both adults who can behave ourselves. We can be professional and polite. If one of us changes our mind or we decide we're just better off as friends, I think we can manage that."

"Okay."

I smile, relieved. And he stares at my mouth for a few seconds before focusing on my eyes again.

"Listen, I already agreed to go see a band in town tomorrow night with some of the guys. It won't be a late night because we've all got work the next morning. But I was wondering if that was the sort of thing you might be interested in coming along with me to?"

Wow. He just asked me on a date. And if feels nice. Natural, actually. Plus, I realize I really do want to spend time with him when I'm not just staring at his hotness. "Sure. That sounds great."

"Good."

I smile. I have a lot to smile about. He likes me. We're doing this. How exciting.

He leans forward. "Can I kiss you, Jude?" he whispers.

I feel those words in every part of me. "Yeah." I lick my

lips. "You can."

As pretty as he was at a distance, he's even more handsome close up. All of the shadows and lines of his face. It blows my mind how Lena left him for another. What a fool. Though I am kind of deeply grateful that she did. His lips are divine. No other word will do. And the thought of him pressing them against mine is making my stomach do a weird flip-flop thing. His lips are neither thin nor plump, but somewhere in between and perfect. I stare at them as he comes closer until he's pressing his mouth softly against mine.

A sweet kiss, as if he's testing his welcome. The man needn't have bothered. I balance on the balls of my feet and join our lips once more, kissing him more insistently. I mean, we might as well figure out here and now if we have no chemistry. If he has no expertise. Because I kissed this male model once who was a tongue-wrangling disaster. Just a whole lot of wet-faced yuck. Sad, but true. It's not like I have kissed anyone in ages. Maybe I've forgotten how it all works. Perhaps I'll be the disaster.

Dean's hands grip my hips, and his tongue slips into my mouth and *oh, yeah*. Very nice. A lack of chemistry is obviously not going to be a problem between us. He kisses me deep and wet in a way that goes straight to my head. My fingers slide over the smooth warm skin of his shoulders before holding on tight. He is so solid and strong. One of his hands is now cupping the back of my head, holding me to him. As if I had any intention of leaving. Heck no. We kiss until my lips are numb and swollen and my mind is far away. Nothing else matters but this moment.

He leans his forehead against mine, and we both take a moment to catch our breath. As first kisses go, it was stellar. My empty stomach, however, shows no cool and rumbles loudly. Talk about keeping it real.

He smiles and kisses my nose, checking out my selection of snacks on the kitchen counter. "Mind if I join you for some middle of the night pickle, turkey, and cheese?"

"Not at all. There will even be Oreos for dessert." I lick my lips and taste him. Nirvana. "You know, you don't have to sleep on the couch. It can't be that comfortable. I don't mind sharing my bed with you if you want."

For a long moment, he just looks at me, his fingers flexing on my hips. Like he's waging some sort of internal war with himself or something. The heat in his gaze lets me know he definitely wants, but he's holding himself back. Which is smart. This thing between us is moving fast. Or at least my hopes and dreams are.

"I didn't necessarily mean it like...you know."

"There's nothing I'd like better than being in your bed. But as you said, we haven't even known each other a day. How about I stay on the couch for now?"

"Okay," I say. "That sounds very wise."

He presses another swift kiss to my lips. "But thank you for offering, Jude. Now let's get you fed."

\* \* \* \*

Frankie is sitting on the sofa the next morning busy with her cell. Her hair is in a perfect chignon, and she's wearing cowboy boots, jeans, and a cream sweater. I don't even own any nice clothing in light colors. It stains too easily. As my misadventure with Anne's silk shirt last night amply displayed. But the woman looks amazing despite it being early. Her makeup is sublime. I am beyond curious as to why Dean doesn't want to date her. Though I acknowledge it's none of my business. Mostly.

Also of note is how Frankie's bags are sitting by the door.

"Hey, Jude," she sing-songs. The woman is obviously a fan of The Beatles. "Dean was telling me I owe you an apology for last night. For not only gate crashing but actually stealing your food. I was starving, sorry. Didn't even think twice."

"It's fine." I fill a mug with coffee. "Are you heading out?"

She makes a comic sad face. "I might as well since Dean doesn't want to get back together again. I knew I should have taken him at his word when he called it off last time. He was using his serious face and somber voice and everything. But I had something else on my mind and I thought he'd get over it and here we are. One day I'll learn. We've been on and off for a while. At the end of the day, however, our lifestyles don't really mesh."

I sip my coffee and stay silent.

"I'm like, let's go! My friends are sailing around the Mediterranean then partying in Ibiza before going shopping in Paris and hitting a movie premiere in London," she says. "As my mom said, I am a force of nature. Not everyone can keep up with me. Nor do they always want to."

"I'm sorry it didn't work out."

She gives me a wink. "No, you're not. And that's okay. We're all adults here. I wish you and him all the best."

"Thanks," I say. Honestly, I'm a little surprised by her non-bitchy attitude. I don't think I could be as cool after losing someone like Dean. I'm not sure whether to be impressed or sad for her.

"Time for me to go." She rises and heads for her luggage. "When he gets out of the shower, tell him I said goodbye."

"You don't want to tell him yourself?"

Frankie shakes her head. "I hate this part. You do it for me."

"Okay."

"Your bangs are so cute. Not everyone can pull off that look."

I lift a hand in farewell. "Thank you, Frankie. Bye."

And the supermodel exits the building. Huh. This week is really not turning out anything like I thought it would. From the outset, it seemed quite boring and normal. But here we are. I put some Pop-Tarts in the toaster and take a breath.

Those kisses with Dean last night were lovely. And his offer to take me to see a band tonight was even lovelier. We spent an hour eating random foods from the fridge and pantry while talking about anything and everything. One of the finest hours I have spent with someone in recent memory.

"Is she gone?" asks the man in question, peeking around the door to the second bedroom.

"Yeah. She just left. She told me to tell you goodbye."

He nods and steps into the living space.

"Any particular reason you were hiding around the corner?"

"I was just testing the waters. She hates goodbyes. They make her cry, and then her eye makeup gets messed up, and she hates that. But sometimes she changes her mind."

"You know each other really well. She seems nice."

"Mm. She is nice. And we know each other well enough to say that we don't really work." He's dressed in black jeans and a matching Henley. "Everything okay with you?"

"Sure."

"By that"—he grins—"I mean, have you changed your mind or are we still on for tonight?"

"No," I say. "We're still on for tonight. Unless you've changed your mind?"

"Nope," he says, licking his lips and making my thighs clench. Without a doubt, he still has my hormones' full and complete attention. This time, the smile he gives me is slow and intimate in the very best way. "I'm looking forward to it."

"Me too. All right then." And there go my loins again. Yikes. I honestly don't know if the way I react to him is due to my being so out of practice with this sort of thing or if he just generally gets to me like no other. "By the way, Frankie talked to me a little about you. How you two didn't work out due to her active lifestyle. Just so you know."

"She loves traveling and socializing. It's her happy place."

"Whereas I am the exact opposite and in dire need of

getting a life."

He cocks his head and says nothing.

"Ah, I didn't mean to…"

"You didn't mean to what?" he asks.

"I just wonder if you're going to get bored hanging out with me."

The smile he gives me is so *warm,* for want of a better word. "You're not boring, Jude. I never know what's going to come out of your mouth, for one thing. It keeps me on my toes. But I'm also okay with not hitting three different parties a night, if you know what I mean."

"I think I do."

"Maybe you'll be bored with me." He winks.

"I doubt that."

"One step at a time, yeah?" He slides his arms around my middle and pulls me in against him for a hug. "We'll just see where this goes."

I wrap my arms around his neck. Our bodies fit together so perfectly. It must be a good sign. I refuse to see it as anything less. "Okay."

\* \* \* \*

When I open the door to the main house at eight a.m., it is to an unusual scene. Dave is holding Jamesy as Evelyn and Lena sit ready and waiting to rapid fire questions at me. About Dean. And Frankie. And everything. Whoa.

"How did your date go?" asks Ev.

Lena holds up a hand. "What was Frankie like? I would kill to photograph her. She has such a fresh take on a classic look. I would go introduce myself, but security said she already left. Did you even get to start on dinner before she showed up last night?"

From the cell sitting on the kitchen table comes Anne's voice saying, "Did his ex ruin everything or not? Wait. No,

Tommy. We don't eat dog biscuits. Put that down. Hey. Come back here. Shit. I mean, shoot. Text me the tea, Ev. I've got to go."

"You got it," says Ev, ending the call.

What with me wanting to keep my job, I head over to Dave first and ask, "Would you like me to take the baby?"

"Sure," he says, giving his son a kiss before he hands him over.

The strange thing is, even after giving me the child, David Ferris doesn't leave for the studio and the day's work. Hell no. He ties his long dark hair back in a ponytail and stands behind his wife, proceeding to massage her shoulders. Like a good partner. Then he tips his chin at me as if I should proceed with my debriefing of the previous night. While it's one thing for me to indulge in a little girl talk, David and Dean have to work together. This is so weird. And some part of these feelings must show on my face.

"You know how smug married couples sometimes get bored and start setting up their friends?" asks Lena. "Meddling in their lives and generally making themselves unwelcome? This is what you're experiencing right now."

"It's true." Ev nods. "It was actually Dave's idea to give you a gentle nudge in the direction of Dean."

I am so surprised I don't know what to say.

But Dave just shrugs. "You're both great people. It just made sense. Though I also felt kind of bad for him after the way things went down with Lena and Jimmy."

"That was years ago," cries Lena. "And it's not like I was mean to him or led him on or anything. At least, I didn't mean to. Stop picking on me. It was complicated, Dave. Sheesh. Be the worst, why don't you? Embrace that lifestyle."

Dave just smiles.

"Huh. Okay. Guess it should be okay to share the basic details since everyone is already involved. To be honest, last night initially did not go well," I say. "I still had trouble talking to him because I was so nervous and my brain kept stalling. The four-inch booties took some practice to walk in too. Then, when we were sitting down on the sofa eating, I fumbled my chop sticks and accidentally dropped a piece of sushi and stained the front of Anne's silk shirt. Though I think I've got it out, thank goodness."

"Oh, no," says Ev.

"Hate it when that happens," mutters Dave.

Lena just nods glumly.

Jamesy happily sucks on his fist while I rock him back and forth. He cares approximately nothing for my dating woes. Which is as it should be.

"Then Frankie arrived out of nowhere, and I was like holy heck," I say. "Because she definitely wanted him back. How was I supposed to compete with a supermodel?"

"I can relate," says Lena. "Jimmy was dating an A-List actress before me, and she was so beautiful. It was terrifying."

Dave's brows draw tight together. "Lena, I've never seen you scared."

"Duh. That's the kind of stuff girls keep hidden."

"This is true," agrees Ev. "We usually do our best to put on a brave face when confronted with competition. Like when I first turned up at the house in L.A. and you had that gorgeous girl in a string bikini surgically attached to you."

"I don't remember anything about that," says Dave with a solid blank face.

"Sure you don't." Ev snorts. "What happened after that, Jude?"

And David Ferris turns back to me and waits patiently for me to continue. Yes. I am dropping details regarding my private life in front of a world-famous musician. I wonder if this is going to wind up in a song or something. The sad and silly dating adventures of Jude the obscure nanny. Hopefully it'll be something with a solid bassline so that it wins hearts and hips on the dance floor.

"She asked if she and Dean could have some privacy. So I just went to my room and went to sleep," I say. "I mean, what else was I going to do?"

Dave sighs. "That sucks it didn't work out, Jude."

"Wait," says Lena. "We're forgetting the part where the supermodel left this morning. And when our fair Jude walked into this room, she was smiling. I sense that there is more to this tale."

"This is where things take yet another turn," I say. "I got up in the middle of the night because I was hungry, and he was sleeping on the couch."

Ev claps, and Jamesy joins in with a gummy grin. "That's my boy," she coos. "Look at your beautiful smile. Keep going, Jude. We need to know all of the details."

"We talked, and he invited me to go see a band with him tonight. If you don't need me, of course."

"We don't need you," says Dave, leaning down to give his wife a kiss. "Right. Good work, everybody. Later."

Evelyn gives me a grin. "You don't know him that well, but that's him practically reveling in your success. He'll be trying to matchmake all of our single friends from now on."

"So," says Lena, "what are you going to wear tonight? We have a couple of other outfits that we put aside on the off chance they were needed. And don't worry too much about the top. Our housekeeper is magic at removing stains. I swear the man made a deal with the devil in exchange for unholy domestic powers. He is a godsend."

I set the baby down, and he races for the nearest toy. A set of bright stacking rings. Jamesy tends to suck on them as opposed to actually stacking them. But a baby's got to do what a baby's got to do.

"I don't know," I say. "As much as I appreciate your help. I think maybe I would be less nervous in my own clothing. Like I would just feel more myself."

"Makes sense to me," agrees Ev.

"Me too." Lena smiles. "I need to get going. I've got a shoot on the other side of town. However, I will look forward to seeing you tonight, Jude."

"You're coming to watch the band?"

"I sure am."

"Thanks again to both of you and Anne for all of your help yesterday," I say. "I really did appreciate it. I doubt I would have had the confidence to attempt doing anything with Dean for ages if you hadn't been encouraging and cheering me on."

Ev just smiles. "Any time."

# Chapter Four

We trade details about our childhoods on the trip into town. I had forgotten how much fun it is getting to know someone new. Hearing all of their stories and sharing my own. These details include our favorite Halloween costumes: a nine-year-old Wolverine for him and a five-year-old hotdog for me. (They were my favorite food at the time.) When we had our first kiss: at age eleven in a cupboard at a party for him and after school at sixteen for me.

The thrill of wanting to know every last little detail about someone is so invigorating. The joy of being out at night and feeling like I have my own life separate from my work is nothing less than a sheer delight. It is as if some weight has been lifted that I wasn't even aware of carrying. Life is so strange. How you can get so busy doing various things and not even notice what's fallen by the wayside. Like actually having a life.

But we both choose to be here together and are enjoying each other's company. How lovely.

The bar is in an old building near the Art Museum. Dean, of course, drives a cool dude sleek silver Porsche 911. Given how low to the ground it is, wearing jeans is working out well for me so far. My brown booties are a slightly more manageable two inches high, and my cute, fitted sweater is dark blue. Chances are, if I spill anything tonight, it won't be as visible. Not that I intend to spill anything. I am nervous, but not as bad as the night before for some reason. Guess it's because I have more of an idea of where I stand with the man. My hair is in a high ponytail, and my makeup worked out well. When I walked out of my room, Dean did a double-take. Then he gave me the slowest, hottest smile in all of creation. A worthwhile thing to do would be to catalogue his smiles. So many of his moods show through them. Or maybe I'm just obsessed.

But I can do this. I can date someone who is cool.

And I believe this, right up until we approach the table where Jimmy and Lena are waiting. Oh no. Jimmy Ferris. My fangirl kryptonite in the flesh. It's like I'm fourteen with bad acne hiding out in my bedroom at home all over again. The decidedly not cool kid who never got invited anywhere. But I had plenty of big dreams. So much yearning.

I resist the urge to giggle and sigh. Just the sight of him brings all of my fourteen-year-old nerves roaring back to life. It's not even attraction so much as it's being in the presence of a real-life rock star. This needs to stop. Now.

Dean pulls out a chair for me, and I give him a nervous smile. Maybe if I just don't look at Jimmy for the remainder of the night, I won't embarrass myself. It might work.

"Hey, guys," says Lena with a broad smile. She, of course, looks amazing. Her dark hair is hanging in long loose curls, and her sweater dress is siren red. I can't help but admire the way she goes through life loud and proud and with such style. When I grow up, I want to be just like her.

"Hi," I say, picking up the menu. A perfect aid for blocking out any views of the elder Ferris brother.

Beside me, Dean pauses before taking his seat and giving Lena a nod. Which is interesting.

A close protection officer stands nearby, keeping an eye on everything. It must be so strange being rich and famous. Having people standing guard over you. The lack of privacy would have to get to you now and then. But I guess it's part of the price you pay for fame and fortune. We're situated near a back exit just in case the crowd gets rowdy or if fans start to flock. No wonder some celebrities hide away in their mansions. I'm not even anyone important, and it's taken me a while to get used to all of the attention and security over the years. The way you can feel all of the eyes on you. Like we're an exhibition at the zoo or something. A couple of people who pull out cells and point them our way are talked to by waiters or management. But most of the bar's patrons are content to just sneak looks now and then. Stage Dive has been living in Portland for a while now. Seeing them around and about isn't unusual. And the proudly weird residents of the city are generally pretty cool.

"Something came up last minute with Lizzy's work, so Ben won't be joining us," says Jimmy.

Dean grimaces. "That's a pity."

"Hey, Jude." Jimmy tips his chin at me. Dammit. I'm not supposed to be looking at the man. "How are you?"

I duck down behind my menu once more. "Good, thank you."

Dean turns to me and says, "Ask me another get-to-know-you question."

"Um," I say, gathering my thoughts. "What was your favorite book as a child?"

"Good question. My father used to read *The Hobbit* to me at bedtime. He was a roadie, so he was away a lot for work. But whenever he was home, he'd read to me. I've got a lot of great memories attached to that book."

"It is a great book." I start to relax a little. "So being in the music business is in your blood?"

"Yeah," he says. "I guess it is. What was your favorite book?"

"*A Wrinkle in Time*," I answer instantly.

"Why that one?"

"Not only was it about a girl going on an adventure, it was the message that you could be yourself and think for yourself, and that was okay. And they told her to stay angry. Not many books tell girls that being angry can be useful and good and right."

He nods. "I'll have to read it."

"I'll be interested to hear what you think. Maybe we could do a buddy read."

"Absolutely." He grins.

The bar is called Felon's and has battered wooden chairs gathered around small, round tables. Patrons have signed their names and the date they were here on the white walls. Poetry and jokes sit alongside some pretty epic works of art. I wonder what they'll do when the walls are covered. If they'll paint over all of it and start again. Low lighting shines down, illuminating the neat rows of liquor bottles behind the bar and the stage situated against the back wall. A drum kit, amps, and microphones stand ready and waiting. No idea when the last time was I saw live music. Apart from watching the Stage Dive guys messing around at home. My life really can seem like a fever dream some days.

A charcuterie board loaded with cheeses, meats, dips, pickled vegetables, and ciabatta is set on the table. It's all adult food. Nothing mashed or pureed in sight. And I cannot wait for it to get in my belly.

"Would you like to order a drink?" asks the waiter.

"The daquiri, thanks," I say from behind my menu.

"I'll have the same." Dean shifts his chair closer to me.

"Why did you never ask me what my favorite childhood book was?" Lena loads up a piece of bread with meat and cheese. "I don't remember you asking me things like that when we were courting."

Jimmy's dark brows descend. Such rock star brows.

Seriously. "Courting?"

"You know what I mean."

"Mm." His tongue plays behind his cheek. "Good question. I don't know. Guess we were too busy fu–"

Lena's hand covers her husband's mouth, ensuring that the rest of the sentence is a garbled mess. "Oh my God. This is why we can't have nice things, Jimmy."

He moves her hand and smiles. "That's not true. You're still the nicest thing I've ever seen."

"Aw. Good save."

"Thanks," he says, smacking a kiss on her cheek.

I can't help but smile. They're so cute together. Not that I should be looking in his direction. *Stop. Bad Jude.* My teenage crush seems to be slumbering at present. But you never know what might wake the beast. It is safest to just keep my gaze averted.

Dean gives the pair a long look before blinking and turning back to me. "Jude. Hey. How you doing?"

"Fine."

The band walks out onto the stage, and the crowd cheers. In no time at all, live rock music fills the room. They're a three piece with a drummer, guitarist, and a female lead singer who also plays the bass. The sound is sort of spare and moody with the singer reminding me a little of Phoebe Bridgers.

"Why this band?" I ask, leaning closer to be heard over the music.

"Ben liked working with Adam Dillon so much, he's looking to do it again. The whole band wants to help and do some mentoring." He rests his arm on the back of my chair, and his lips brush against my ear now and then as he speaks, making shivers run down my spine. "They asked me to come tonight and see what I thought of this group. As for why…they're talented. They've got a good sound, and the audience is into them. I think with the right help, they could go far. What do you think of them?"

"So far so good."

"Is this okay?" he asks, nodding to his arm and so on.

"Yes." It's much more than okay, if I'm being honest. And the way he looks at me. I am such a fool for this man. "What are you thinking about, Jude?"

"I was, ah…just happy to be here."

"Good," he says. "Me too. Of course, what this band really needs is someone playing the flute."

"Right?" I grin. "I could totally help them. This one time at band camp…"

His shoulders shake as he laughs. "I can't believe you went there."

"Please. You love it." Our drinks arrive, and I thank the waiter and take a sip. "Yummy."

His gaze moves past me and pauses on Lena. Just for a moment. Then his attention returns to me and my curious face. He studies me for more than a moment. "You know that Lena and I went out a couple of times way back when," he asks. But it's not really a question. He already knows the answer. "This is the first time we've been around each other for more than a minute or two."

"Is this uncomfortable for you?"

He shakes his head. "That was a long time ago, and it's not like we were serious. She was already in love with Jimmy, I just didn't know it. Taught me a valuable lesson about not dating someone whose heart is already spoken for."

I'm happy to hear him say that but can't help myself from asking the question that's been on my mind since last night. "And Frankie definitely doesn't have yours?"

His gaze narrows on me just so. "No. She doesn't."

"Ignore me," I say. "I shouldn't have said anything. You already told me that—"

One side of his mouth lifts up. "Jude, it's okay. Frankie is great. I hope we'll always be friends. But I promise you, there's nothing more going on. I know we only just met each other. But I'm going to prove to you that you can trust me."

"Okay."

"Guess I should be checking your heart is also free."

"It most definitely is."

"That's good to hear. Did you ever think you'd be double dating with Lena and Jimmy Ferris?"

I softly laugh. "Not even a little."

"Me neither." He lowers his face and sniffs my neck. And he's not even subtle about it. "How do you smell so amazing?"

"Would you like the truth?"

"Always."

I smile and shift in my seat. Because being closer to him seems like a great idea to me. It's like we're in our own little bubble of infinite possibility. And it is beautiful. "This is a distinctly unsexy answer, but it's probably Jamesy's organic diaper balm or the calming lavender lotion I put on him."

"The baby needs calming?"

"Most of them do at one stage or another."

"What's that like, working with children?" he asks.

"It's fun and challenging. Sometimes a little bit hellish. But what job isn't?"

"This is true," he says. "It's not unknown for rock stars to act like toddlers now and then. But I don't have a lot of experience with children in general."

"Watching them grow and learn can be amazing. They develop so quickly in those first few years. Not just going from crawling to walking, but language and comprehension too. They're kind of fascinating."

"I can see that." He turns back to the band, listening as they change to a folksier-sounding song. "How did you get into working with celebrities?"

"I was finishing a degree in early childhood development,

and a friend's sister worked as a personal assistant for someone big in Hollywood." In an act of sheer bravery, I take hold of his hand. Underneath the table and out of sight, our fingers entwine. His hand is large and the tips of his fingers lightly callused. From playing the guitar, probably. It's nice to hold someone's hand again. To feel connected to a special person in a such a sweet way. "She heard that they were after someone young but qualified who could be trusted not to spill any secrets. It wasn't what I was planning on doing, but the money was good, and the idea of being around people like that was intriguing. They traveled a lot too, and that was cool. I hadn't been many places beyond the West Coast. What about you? Was it the link with your father that got you into producing?"

He nods. "He took me to shows with him when he could. Bought me my first guitar when I was seven or so."

"What were your biggest influences besides your dad?"

"Music-wise, I like all sorts of styles. Mom had varied tastes and a great collection of vinyl. She liked playing The Pixies, Placebo, Sister Rosetta Tharpe, Ray Charles...I could go on all night."

"I feel like we need to have a listening to music date. Not that this isn't," I say. "You know what I mean. Were you ever interested in being in a band yourself?"

"Nah." He gives my hand a squeeze. "I prefer working behind the scenes. Touring for months on end isn't really my thing. Getting hassled every time you go out..."

And it is funny he should say that because a beautiful woman is creeping up to his side with a piece of paper in hand. The bodyguard watches but doesn't intervene. It's not like she's approaching Jimmy or Lena. But he does keep his eye on the stranger. She gives Dean a tentative smile and ignores me entirely.

"Excuse me," she says. "Are you Dean Jennings, the producer who worked on The Sugar Bowl's last record?"

"Yeah, I am."

Her answering smile is broad as can be. "Oh my God. That album was amazing. What you did really elevated their sound."

"Thanks."

It's the way Dean's body language abruptly changes that bothers me. He releases my hand and turns away from me. Just enough to exclude me from the conversation. Not that I was a part of it to begin with because what do I even know about producing music? Nothing. It might be my imagination, but it feels like he doesn't want to be seen with me. I don't know. Any time I've been out on dates in the past, being suddenly ignored is rarely a good sign. And I highly doubt that has changed.

Even Lena is frowning in our direction. It's not just me and my imagination. Okay.

Jimmy meanwhile keeps watching the band, spellbound by the music and oblivious to the drama. Not a bad way to be. The band really is great. I hope they have the opportunity to get their music out to people.

Dean and the mysterious stranger start chatting, and she tells him all about the music she's been making. She sings, plays guitar, and writes her own songs. Wish I was that talented. My singing voice is best confined to the car or shower. Though my rendition of "Bad Guy" by Billie Eilish is solid. Just take my word. I can't catch much of the conversation due to the noise, but Dean seems totally engrossed. He doesn't even spare me a glance. It appears that these two have a lot in common. Not to mention, the woman who is slipping him all of her contact details is gorgeous. Her head is shaved, and her cleavage is spectacular. She even has a cool neck tattoo. As if Frankie the supermodel wasn't a big enough hit to my ego.

No. Enough of this negative self-talk. I am great in my own way. As for my chest, I'll never have to worry about developing lower back pain. I can get around sans a bra with little to no visible boob bouncing. There are positives to everything. Maybe.

But right now, I could do with a break from this anxiety-inducing situation.

"Back in a minute," I say to a still frowning Lena. How Dean is failing to feel her eyes boring a hole into the side of his skull, I have no idea. But the woman has my back, which is nice to know. Meeting great people through my position with the Ferris family has been a boon that I hugely appreciate.

I head down a hallway to the bathrooms and see to business before washing my hands. It is nice to be out of sight of anyone for a moment. The muffled music thrums through the walls, but it's quieter back here. I can collect my thoughts and put things into perspective. And the fact is, I still feel weird about the way Dean gave me the cold shoulder and dismissed me. Without even so much as an *excuse me* or whatever. I don't want to be treated that way. My mother raised me to believe that manners matter. My father taught me that some people will behave as badly as they can get away with. Sad but true.

Am I also letting my jealousy get the better of me? I don't know. It's not as if I have any claim over Dean. Though other people looking at him with bedroom eyes does not make me happy. Jealousy hasn't been a huge issue in any of my previous dating attempts. At least, I don't think it has.

When I walk out of the bathroom, it's to find Dean waiting for me. The man remains every bit as built and handsome as before. He leans against the wall with his hands in his pockets and his foot tapping to the music. He lifts his head and gives me a warm smile. But I'm not quite feeling the magic.

He takes a step closer. "Hey."

I give him a pleasant smile. "Hi."

At which point, he stops and stares at me. Then his dark brows descend. The man is no longer happy. "Lena was right."

"About what?"

He nods to the far end of the hallway, farther away from the music and anyone who might wander this way. The light is also dimmer down here. If this isn't prime make-out territory, then I don't know what is. Not that I'm here for those reasons. For the first time since I met Dean my libido has shut down. The needy beast sleeps once more. Which is probably for the best.

"Lena said I was a dick to turn my back on you to talk to that woman the way I did," he says. "That I wasn't treating you with respect."

I say nothing.

His frown increases tenfold. It's quite a sight to see. Then he walks forward, not stopping until I am backed up against the nearest wall. They way he looms over me is a lot.

"Dean." I put a hand to his chest. "That's enough."

"I'm sorry you thought I was being dismissive. That was not my intent."

"What was your intent?"

"I don't get approached a lot like Jimmy or the guys. But it does happen now and then," he says. "I put you behind me and out of her line of vision because I didn't want her attention on you. She's a complete stranger. I don't know if she's going to be cool or not. There's always a small chance she might be dangerous if I don't give her what she wants. People can be wild when it comes to something they feel possibly entitled to."

"Oh," I say, starting to understand that things might not have been what they seemed.

"Did you know someone pushed Anne once to try and get to Mal? Just about shoved her off the sidewalk into traffic. Another reason why I can do without being a rock star." He sets his hands on either side of my head. "But I am known in certain circles. Like tonight, people occasionally want to say hi or compliment me on my work or see if I can aid their rise in the industry."

"Right."

"That's why I turned my back on you. I can understand how me doing that seemed rude as fuck. But please know that it was not my intention. I am out tonight with you, and you are important to me, Jude. I'm not chatting up another woman. This was my way of trying to keep you safe." And he just stares down at me.

"Okay. I guess that all, um, makes sense." I squeeze my eyelids shut tight and take a deep breath. "Here's the thing. It's been a long time since I dated. And my dating history is not the best."

"Give me an example."

"Well," I say, "the last time I was about to meet with someone for the first time, they texted me an hour before to ask if he needed to wear a condom or not."

"Seriously?" He practically growls.

"Oh, yeah. I said wearing a prophylactic out to a coffee shop sounded uncomfortable. But he should of course feel free to do as he pleased."

His jaw clenches. "What did he say?"

"He blocked me." I sigh. "I don't think I missed out on much there."

"I don't think you did either." He seems to get control of his anger towards condom guy. "I'm sorry that happened."

I just shrug. What's there to say? Dating sucks. "Dean, it's been a long time since I've had all of these sorts of feelings for someone. And I know we've only known each other for like a day and a half, but you inspire a lot of emotion in me. I feel like there's a real connection between us. That's the truth."

"Okay," he says in a calm voice. "I feel that too."

"Just so you know, flying into jealous rages isn't my thing. I can adjust to the idea that you used to date a supermodel, and I can get used to people approaching you."

"Good. I'm really glad to hear that." He smiles. "If it makes any difference, I didn't like the way the guy at the next table was staring at you and trying to get your attention."

"The guy at the next table was staring at me?"

"Yeah. He was."

"Huh. I didn't notice." I swallow. "Since we're doing such great communicating and all…I also happened to see you give Lena a couple of pensive glances. I think pensive is the word."

"It's probably the right word." He softly laughs. "Like I said, I really haven't been around her in years. The last time was when she and Jimmy were getting together. And between you and me, they had a fight this one time. It was kind of brutal. Jimmy wound up firing her. Guess I was wondering if she was really happy or not. Not because I am still interested in her as a friend. Just because, you know?"

"That's good of you to care."

"Now do you want to tell me why you were hiding from Jimmy behind the menu?"

"Ugh. You noticed that, did you?"

He just waits. There will be no sudden change of subject to save me, apparently.

"Look, I'm going to be brutally honest with you," I say. "You seem to prefer brutal honesty to prevarication or any other such nonsense. The truth is he was my childhood crush, and seeing him in real life still throws me sometimes. My face goes bright red, and it is horribly embarrassing and stupid, and I wish it would stop."

"Wait." His lips thinned. "You have a crush on Jimmy Ferris?"

"*Had* a crush. When I was a teenager."

Oh, dear. He has very much reverted to his former state of being unhappy. Crankiness fills his gaze. It didn't occur to me that this might be a somewhat sore point for him what with losing Lena to the man. But seriously.

"Dean," I chide. "Haven't you ever met one of your childhood heroes and lost it? Perhaps not repeated, but still…you get what I mean, right?"

He frowns some more and then he sighs. "Rihanna."

"Rihanna?"

"I had a thing for her when I was younger."

I nod encouragingly. "She is amazing."

"Crossed paths with her briefly at an industry thing a while back. I just stuttered some shit and ran away in shame. It was awful."

"This is what I'm saying. It doesn't mean anything. It's just some strange fixation left over from our childhood that we're still working through and has no actual bearing on our adult lives apart from being occasionally embarrassing because it causes us to momentarily regress."

"That was a really long sentence."

"I feel like it hit all of the important points, though."

His gaze narrows on me. "Jude, are you going to get over your Jimmy thing?"

"Yes. Absolutely. Any day now." I wind my arms around his neck. "Guess we both have our sore spots. But look at us communicating like absolute champions. Let's make a deal that we continue to talk things out as soon as possible whenever possible."

"That sounds good. This feels a little like speed dating, the rate at which we're knocking down complicated topics." His hands rest on my hips, and he places a gentle kiss on my lips. "Are we okay?"

"We?"

"Yeah."

My smile barely fits on my face. "We're most definitely okay."

# Chapter Five

We get back to the guest house a little after eleven. It's not exactly a late night, but I am usually in bed by now, wrapped in blankets and reading a romance novel. The initial high of being with someone is so beautiful. Like walking on clouds and feeling your heart take flight and all of those fanciful things. I had forgotten. Or at least I hadn't made time to remember. Life gets busy, and years pass by without you realizing. Without you getting the things you want. And I have decided I would like to be in a relationship. With this man, if possible.

Dean is right, we're speed dating. Part of it is the forced proximity of sharing the guest house. He's right the heck there and will continue to be so each and every night, apparently. The only time we're not around each other is when we're at work. And when we're at work, we're probably both too busy to stop and think all of this through. Which brings us right back to being together and whoa. My heart is beating like a drum while my mind does its best to keep up. All of these hopes and dreams fill up my head at a dizzying rate.

"Thank you for coming out with me tonight," he says in his smooth, deep voice.

"You're very welcome. Thank you for asking me."

"How about tomorrow night, if you don't already have

plans, you pick what we do?"

I smile. "That sounds great."

"It's a date," he says and leans in for a kiss. This one is gentle and tame just like the other he gave me in the hallway back at the bar. There's none of the smoldering heat from the middle of the night. We were all wet mouths and clutching hands then. This is sweet but perfunctory.

Though there's always the chance I'm overthinking things. Again. It must be amazing to have some chill and be good at relationships and dating. Imagine the lack of worrying such a person would do. You could take up a new hobby with all of the time you'd save.

"I'll see you in the morning," he says and heads for his bedroom. When he reaches his door, he raises a hand in farewell.

I return the motion with a hesitant smile.

And then he is gone from view. The door is closed, and our date is over. It was a success, I think.

The house is quiet as can be, and outside, everything is dark. At this hour of night, it seems the whole world is asleep. Or holding its breath waiting for the next thing to happen. Tonight was fine. It was good. We went on a date and, apart from a hiccup, it was great. Said hiccup probably even strengthened our burgeoning relationship when you think about it. I am on the whole content with tonight's events.

I wander into my bedroom, slipping off my shoes and stretching my toes. It's not that I thought he would necessarily try to get into my pants on the first date. But those kisses were a little lackluster. Harsh but true. I know for a fact that he can do better. Instead, he took our heat level down a notch or two. Or three. The woman in the mirror has no answers. I take off my makeup and brush my teeth and change into pajamas. Not even comfortable fluffy socks can solve this quandary.

I lie on my bed in the dark for almost an hour. My brain won't quiet down, and I don't know what to do. Though in all honesty I do know what to do, I'm just not sure if I should do it. Making decisions like this can be a right bitch. My hands curl into fists, and it's all so frustrating. Along with the button to turn the libido on and off, there definitely needs to be one for the brain. A little sleep mode switch behind the ear or something. How useful. I consider going the warm milk and cookie route. But I'm not really hungry, and sugar would probably not help. I can't read for a while because my mind won't focus on anything else. It is all Dean and me town up there. Too many thoughts and feelings going on. Not even a meditation app on my cell can calm me down. It's like I'm in Oregon and sleep is in Maine. No joke. The other side of the country. And no, I am not being needlessly dramatic.

Much.

It takes me a good minute of standing in front of Dean's bedroom door to work up the nerve to knock. Then I start out so softly he would need superpowers to have heard. Ugh. Me. Honestly. I give knocking a less timid attempt and then stand there to wait. If he hadn't figured out I could be complicated and high maintenance now and then, he soon will. Which is probably for the best.

He answers in those sleep pants with a bare chest and feet. Just how does this man expect me to not ogle him? It's impossible. His eyes are sleeping, his dark hair adorably ruffled. He gives me a fond smile as he says, "Jude. Is everything okay?"

"I'm sorry to disturb you, but you said you wanted honesty, and I had a thought that couldn't wait."

"Okay."

"Why did you pull back on the heat level?"

He cocks his head. "Why did I what?"

"Last night in the kitchen we made out and it was great. But tonight it was like I could have been your sister."

"My sister?" He raises his chin. "Trust me when I tell you I do not consider you to be sibling like in any way."

I take a step back. "Okay. Sorry I woke you."

"Wait." He grabs hold of my hand. "Jude, the thing is, I got to thinking, and I thought maybe we should slow down. That I should take the time to woo you properly."

"Oh."

"We're not even at forty-eight hours of knowing each other yet. It is damn tempting knowing you're so close. But I've got this feeling about us. I want it to work." He licks his lips. "Listen to me, in no way at all do I see you as sisterly."

I exhale hard. "Good. That all sounds…good."

"But if we're going to start spending a lot of time together like I hope we are, I don't want you to feel rushed or pressured. Does that make sense?" He rubs the pad of his thumb back and forth over my knuckles. Such fleeting contact. Not a big deal at all. But the sensation seems to run straight through me, setting me alight.

"You've got a good feeling about us?"

"Yes."

"Me too."

"Think you can sleep now?"

I consider the question then shake my head slowly. "No."

He frowns.

"You remember what it was like when you were waiting for Christmas as a child? Trying to sleep the night before was next to impossible. All you could think about was the presents that some strange man with a beard wearing red velvet was going to break into your house and leave underneath the tree. The adrenaline would be pumping and your mind racing and…you know what I mean?"

His smile more than reaches his eyes. "Are you comparing me to Christmas?"

"Yes. And you may not have guessed this about me, but I am impatient. Especially when it comes to you, apparently." I take a deep breath. "The other thing is, if we're not going to work out, I'd rather know sooner than later. It'll hurt less. I mean, we could just not work in bed. It could happen. Just because we have chemistry kissing doesn't mean everything will be great."

"I'm pretty sure it'll be great," he says with all of the arrogance.

"I want proof. Now."

The smile increases to a grin. "That's what you want, huh?"

I nod.

"Are you thinking fucking or making love?" he asks playfully. "Where is this mood of yours at, hmm?"

"Let's start with the first and see how we go."

The man stares down at me in wonder. At least, I choose to believe that's the expression in his eyes. Best just to check, however.

"Do you think I'm being too forward or aggressive?"

"No. Hell no." His brows draw down. "What I was thinking was…I must have done something very right to land me in this moment with you. No idea what it could be. But I am extremely grateful."

I smile back at him.

"Can't believe you think we wouldn't work in bed, though. Not going to lie, Jude. That hurts."

"So prove me wrong, Dean. Prove me wrong." I take off my Henley pajama top, leaving us both bare from the waist up. The way his gaze dips down, over my breasts and belly is delicious indeed. My thighs clench, and I am definitely in need. "Whenever you're ready."

He gazes at me as if I am indeed a hot dream come to life. "Whatever you want, Jude."

Kissing shouldn't be seen as being especially dangerous or a contact sport. But the way we go at it, it just might be. Our mouths meet and meld and oh yes. This was what I wanted. Hot, wet, and all consuming. Tongues tangle and teeth clash. There's no stopping us now that we've started. No slowing down or being sensible. Whatever his thoughts were on taking our time before, he is all in and all over me now.

My hands grip his shoulders before wrapping around his neck. While his coast down my back and over my butt. Polite society may not deem it considerate to climb a person. But Dean has no such problems. Thank goodness. He lifts me, and my legs go around his waist nice and tight. I am the spider monkey equivalent of a woman. No way am I letting go. Still kissing our hearts out, he turns and walks us into his room. I love dragging my fingers through his thick hair. Grabbing a handful and holding on tight. His fingers dig into my thighs, and he groans low in his throat. Quite possibly the hottest sound I have ever heard.

He's already good and hard against me. And I am so wet it is obscene. We haven't even gotten fully naked yet, and this might be the best sex of my life. Seriously. Then he lowers me onto the mattress with a parting kiss. My lips are most definitely wet and swollen. And the taste of him is all mint toothpaste and hot man.

"Are you good to lose your pants?" he asks, his breathing as rapid as mine.

"Yeah."

His fingers hook on the waistband, and with one tug, they're gone. No more than a flannel cotton memory lying on the floor in the corner of the room. Next, my fluffy socks go flying. I am naked as the day I was born. Dean pulls open the top drawer on the bedside table and grabs a box. He swears quietly at the delay when his fingers fumble over the plastic. Then he tears off a condom and sets it on the bed beside me.

"What about your pants?" I ask.

"Soon," is all he says before getting to his knees.

The way he grabs my legs and drags me to the edge of the bed—putting me right where he wants me—it is all more than a little thrilling. His big hands hold my thighs open as he lowers his face to my sex. He breathes me in with a happy sigh. Which makes me a little nervous honestly. But he seems delighted at the scent or me. He wastes no time in nuzzling me and sucking on my labia. Just generally driving me wild. The flat of his tongue drags through my middle and oh boy. How everything in me focuses on those feelings. On the shivers running down my back and the perfect pressure building low in my belly and spine. Can't recall the last time a man went down on me. And the way Dean obviously relishes doing this makes all the difference.

He fucks me with his tongue before teasing me from my clit to my ass. No part of me is left untended. I lie there panting on the bed, my hands fisting the sheets. All the while, he works me higher and higher. The man obviously believes in the woman coming first. And I could honestly salute him for his efforts. By the time he starts sucking my clit in earnest, I am poised to plummet. It's like freefalling into the sky. Like shedding my body and flying. My muscles spasm, and it's all him. His touch and expertise. How much he enjoys this moment. It's obvious in the way his fingers press into my thighs. In how he pauses to whisper words of encouragement now and then. I come against his face, and it is so good. Breathtaking and beautiful. There's every chance I shouted his name to the heavens. But hey...he more than deserves the recognition.

By the time I come back down, he's ditched his pajama pants and is rolling on the condom. He lifts me into the middle of the bed and climbs over my body. His dick is a bit thicker than most I have seen. Which can only mean good things for me. If he knows how to use it. Given his above average oral skills, my hopes are sky high. As previously imagined, his whole body is sublime. I would draw him if I had the least talent. But my basic stick figure capabilities would not do him justice. Not even a little. The muscles in his long legs, his calves, and the thicker thighs. How his hips have those dips that drive me wild. I love the scent of him. A lingering hint of cologne and clean male sweat. There is every chance I will be licking the man asap.

"Are we good?" he asks in a voice deeper than before.

"Yes," I breathe.

Our mouths meet again, and the taste of me on his tongue suits him just fine. I might yet brand the boy with my name. It's not out of the question. All of the good hormones are floating around inside me from the orgasm. I wrap my legs and arms around him and hold on tightly, wanting to have him in me good and deep, both his cock and his tongue. I want to give back to him what he gave to me. Have him come. Make him feel as good as can be.

He lines up the blunt head of his cock and pushes in sure but steady. I gasp at the feel of him. At the slight burn as he stretches me. At the sudden awareness of those recently unused muscles. He groans against my ear and buries his face in my neck. His breath is warm against my skin. It's all so up close and personal, having him against me. This might be our first time, but there's none of the awkward or embarrassing feelings that you might expect. It feels right to have him wrapped up in me.

When he's as deep as he can be, he licks my neck before biting it, before fucking me. Slow, long thrusts at first. But he soon builds up the speed and force. I lock my ankles behind his back and hang on for dear life. He took the request to fuck me seriously. One of his hands slides down my side, gripping my ass cheek nice and tight. My skin is sure to show some small marks tomorrow. And though he tries to kiss me, we're too frantic, our bodies too demanding. I raise my hips with each thrust, meeting him halfway and urging him on. Faster. Deeper. More. The slap of his skin against mine fills the room along with the scent of sex. If I could bottle and keep it I would.

He builds me back up gradually. I don't often come twice. I don't always come at all. But Dean has taken the job of proving we work together in bed to heart, it would seem. And I was a fool to doubt him. The man knows what he's doing. Our bodies fit just fine. I moan and hold on as tightly as can be. While he angles himself to give me that necessary pressure. It is electric, the way he turns me on. How he blows my mind. Everything in me tenses down low and *fuck*.

"That's my good girl," he mutters. "Come on me, Jude. I need to feel you."

And I do. My heart is stuck in my throat, and my body just...goes boom. All of the muscles inside of me clench at his cock and the noise he makes. How he swears and slams himself into me. The man knows how to fuck. I really do owe him an apology. Which I will give just as soon as I come down once again from the heavens. His hips buck, and his cock jerks as he comes. The way he holds on to me so tightly is lovely. Like he might never let me go.

Sweat slicks our skin, and his body lies against mine. I love the weight of him. The solidity of being held down against the mattress by his body this way. Other times I was crowded or anxious after sex, but not with him. With him, I feel safe. My limbs are all limp and melty. Like I just got a really great massage or something. And last but not least, my mind is at ease. Dean is, without a doubt, just what I needed.

"You were right," he mumbles. "We have no chemistry. We absolutely suck in bed."

I reach down to slap him on the ass just because.

He laughs and groans. "How much sleep do you need?"

"Six hours minimum."

"Me too. I say we rest for a bit, then we'll give making love a go."

I grin. "Sounds good."

\* \* \* \*

The next morning, over Pop-Tarts and coffee, it's like we've been dating for a while. We move in sync, sharing small touches and little kisses in the kitchen. Like our bodies are hyper aware of each other and can't stand to be apart for long.

It's just seems so *easy* to fall into life with Dean. And I don't want to fight the pull of this happiness and contentment.

Last night, he definitely fucked me. But around 4 a.m., we made love. Slow. Gentle. He kissed every part of my body he could find. Like he was worshiping me. Us. And something shifted in my brain. Instead of wondering if I was doing anything wrong, or if he was thinking of anyone else, I just…let go.

I know he felt it. The change. Because his reverence turned to obsession. Like he couldn't get enough. Of my taste. My touch. And when I whispered his name with my last orgasm, he plunged deep, hugged me hard, and sighed my name with his release.

He held me until morning and woke me with a smile and a kiss. Along with a cup of coffee.

Extra points for the coffee.

We showered together, which is a new experience I intend to repeat, and then dressed for the day.

"See you tonight," he says on his way out, a small smile playing at his lips when he kisses me. "Don't play too hard with the toddler."

"Don't worry." I wink. "I intend to save my playtime for you."

Yes, I'm corny. But that's me.

And by the heated look he gives me, he likes me just fine.

# Epilogue

*One month later...*

"This is ridiculous," I say, standing in the middle of the living room of the main house. Like an idiot.

Jimmy grunts his agreement. As he should.

"No negativity allowed," announces Malcolm Ericson.

Meanwhile, my loving boyfriend, Dean Jennings, just shrugs and smiles as he leans against the wall. He is totally enjoying this. The jerk. I totally take back my admission of love from a few nights ago. Though he's not allowed to recant his. For reasons.

This was meant to be a get-together to celebrate them wrapping production on the new album. A very pregnant Anne is seated on the couch along with Lizzy and Ben. While Ev and David stand arm in arm in front of the fireplace. And Lena is pouring herself another glass of champagne from the selection of food and drink on the coffee table. All of the children are elsewhere for the occasion. As cute and fun as they are, it's nice to have an adults-only night.

"Jude, face your nemesis, please," says Mal.

I groan and turn back to the lead singer of Stage Dive, who is standing a full two feet away from me. Which is scarily close. The thing is, it turns out that my hideous teenage crush on

Jimmy is the worst kept secret in existence. I don't know exactly what they do in the recording studio. But gossiping definitely happens. The whole band and my boyfriend have been spilling the tea. And apparently, the person they have been gossiping about is me. Oh, the freaking shame of it all.

"Are we done yet?" asks Jimmy, flicking back his dark hair in a move worthy of the big screen. Though it lacks the dynamite sex appeal of when Dean does it. Harsh but true.

"No." Lena retakes her seat on the couch. "We're helping our friends. Stay there and do as you're told!"

Jimmy just sighs.

"Sorry about this," I mumble.

"It's not exactly you're fault."

I turn to give my boyfriend a death glare.

To which he smiles and waves. "You're doing great, babe."

But Mal is not happy. "Stop distracting her, Dean. They're meant to be staring at each other. This is serious immersive therapy we've got going on here. Right, Lizzy?"

"Immersion therapy," says Lizzy. "But close enough."

"That's what I said."

I stare at Jimmy. The grimace he gives me looks honestly painful. Poor dude. I think he would rather be sorting socks than standing staring at me. I know I would be. All I did was turn a little pink when I unexpectedly bumped into the man the other day. But Mal saw it and said something, and the menfolk discussed it, and now here we are. Without a doubt, this is one of the most embarrassing situations ever. Hands down. The clear winner. Malcom Ericson is the worst. My least favorite member of Stage Dive. Forever. It may seem harsh, but it is warranted.

"I think I'm good now," I say, giving the audience a thumbs-up.

"No," yells Mal. "Stay there. It hasn't even been two minutes, and we're aiming for at least five."

"Maybe if we pointed out some of his flaws to her that

would be helpful," asks Dave with a bottle of beer in hand and an amused smile on his face. "Like how he has that small scar on his forehead from when he was running through the house as a kid and got distracted and ran into the corner of a wall."

Mal shakes his head sorrowfully.

"Oh. I've got one," says Lena. "His left ear is slightly higher than the other. And he refuses to eat broccoli which everyone knows is the best vegetable."

"It really is," agrees Anne.

"How about how clingy he is with his cars," says Ev. "He just about babies them."

Lena snorts. "He so does."

Jimmy looks to heaven, but he is all out of luck. There is no help forthcoming. Not from on high and not from in here.

"He stole the last donut from the box the other morning," says Dean. "Didn't even ask if anyone else wanted it."

"Where are your manners, dude?" Mal frowns. "That's awful. I would never do that."

"Yes you would," says Anne. "You were teaching Tommy to grab the last cookie and run and hide just the other week."

"Pumpkin. We're all picking on Jimmy right now. This is no time for the truth."

Anne sags back against the sofa, rubbing her ginormous belly. "Whatever."

"I really do think I'm good now," I say.

"Good is a strong word." Mal steps closer and peers at me. "Good would be your crush transferring to a more suitable person such as myself. Talented, good-looking, I've got it all. You wouldn't believe how amazing I am. I mean, check out my long blond hair. Beautiful, right?"

"Um. Yeah. It's great, Mal."

"Right? Better even than Chris Hemsworth when he's playing Thor. I told him that, and he nearly cried. The dude is much more delicate than you'd expect for someone that size. But back to me. Let me demonstrate my hair for you." Mal tosses his hair this way and that. "See what I mean? Look at that color and movement. And the texture is so soft."

"Wow."

He stops swishing his hair about and studies my face instead. Which I could definitely do without. Then he says, "But as for your thing for Jimmy, I'm not seeing any sign of lingering signs of fangirl behavior. No dreaminess in the eyes. Your hands aren't even shaking with excitement at his presence. Though you are a little pink in the cheeks still."

"I think that might be due to current circumstances than any lingering teenage crush," says Lizzy. "Having her stand in the middle of the room while we all watch and comment would be a lot for most anyone."

Mal shrugs. "I would have no problem with that, thank you very much."

"Yeah," says Ben. "But you're not normal. Have you noticed that?"

"Shut up, Ben. Nobody was talking to you."

The big man just shrugs.

Jimmy makes a growly noise and pulls me into a hug. It is basically him patting me on the back with a vaguely pained expression. "Okay, Jude. We're all good."

"Thanks, Jimmy."

"But it hasn't been five minutes," cries Mal.

Jimmy ruffles his hair. "Move on, man."

"Don't mess with the hair."

Dean wanders over and pulls me into his arms. The smile on his face...he is much too damn amused by all of this. I should step on his toes. But I am a wonderful, forgiving woman. So I wrap my arms around his waist and hide my face against his chest for a moment. Because Lizzy was right, that was a lot.

"I thought you were brave facing down your crush like that," says Dean in a low voice.

"This better be the last I ever hear about it. Or else."

"Fair enough." He kisses me on the head and rubs my back. "I love you, Jude."

"I love you too."

We have decided to try long distance for a while. At least for the next few months to a year. Having Dean welcome to stay with me in the guest house whenever he can will make things easier. There's a studio in town that he likes working at too. He doesn't always have to be in L.A. And he's in sufficient demand to ask the talent to come to him. I have no idea what the future will bring. But after the last month, I am hopeful that we have a long future ahead of us. We've spent every night and weekend together. Going out to restaurants and listening to bands and watching TV. Just being happy together and working through things.

I've never felt this way about anyone, and he feels the same. We're committed to making this work.

I didn't even realize something was missing, but his love is just what I needed.

\* \* \* \*

Also from Kylie Scott and 1001 Dark Nights, discover Rhythm Method, Love Song, Closer, and Strong.

Sign up for the 1001 Dark Nights Newsletter
and be entered to win a Tiffany Key necklace.

There's a contest every month!

Go to www.1001DarkNights.com to subscribe.

**As a bonus, all subscribers can download**
**FIVE FREE exclusive books!**

# Discover 1001 Dark Nights Collection Nine

DRAGON UNBOUND by Donna Grant
A Dragon Kings Novella

NOTHING BUT INK by Carrie Ann Ryan
A Montgomery Ink: Fort Collins Novella

THE MASTERMIND by Dylan Allen
A Rivers Wilde Novella

JUST ONE WISH by Carly Phillips
A Kingston Family Novella

BEHIND CLOSED DOORS by Skye Warren
A Rochester Novella

GOSSAMER IN THE DARKNESS by Kristen Ashley
A Fantasyland Novella

DELIGHTED by Lexi Blake
A Masters and Mercenaries Novella

THE GRAVESIDE BAR AND GRILL by Darynda Jones
A Charley Davidson Novella

THE ANTI-FAN AND THE IDOL by Rachel Van Dyken
A My Summer In Seoul Novella

CHARMED BY YOU by J. Kenner
A Stark Security Novella

THE CLOSE-UP by Kennedy Ryan
A Hollywood Renaissance Novella

DESCEND TO DARKNESS by Heather Graham
A Krewe of Hunters Novella

BOND OF PASSION by Larissa Ione
A Demonica Novella

JUST WHAT I NEEDED by Kylie Scott
A Stage Dive Novella

THE SCRAMBLE by Kristen Proby
A Single in Seattle Novella

*Also from Blue Box Press*

THE BAIT by C.W. Gortner and M.J. Rose

THE FASHION ORPHANS by Randy Susan Meyers and M.J. Rose

TAKING THE LEAP by Kristen Ashley
A River Rain Novel

SAPPHIRE SUNSET by Christopher Rice writing as C. Travis Rice
A Sapphire Cove Novel

THE WAR OF TWO QUEENS by Jennifer L. Armentrout
A Blood and Ash Novel

THE MURDERS AT FLEAT HOUSE by Lucinda Riley

THE HEIST by C.W. Gortner and M.J. Rose

SAPPHIRE SPRING by Christopher Rice writing as C. Travis Rice
A Sapphire Cove Novel

MAKING THE MATCH by Kristen Ashley
A River Rain Novel

A LIGHT IN THE FLAME by Jennifer L. Armentrout
A Flesh and Fire Novel

# Discover More Kylie Scott

### The Rhythm Method: A Stage Dive Novella

It all started in Vegas...

After a wild and tumultuous beginning to their relationship, Evelyn Thomas and her rock star husband David Ferris have been happily married for years. Nothing needs to change, their life together is perfect. Which means that change in the shape of an unexpected pregnancy is bound to shake things up some. But could it be for the better?

\* \* \* \*

### Love Song: A Stage Dive Novella

There's always the one that got away. Or kicked you out...

The new darling of rock 'n' roll, Adam Dillon, is ready to show his ex-girlfriend, Jill Schwartz, what a mistake she made kicking him to the curb. So maybe he wasn't the best of boyfriends. Writing great songs and climbing to the top of the charts isn't easy. Only problem is, he's fast finding out that success isn't everything.

\* \* \* \*

### Closer: A Stage Dive Novella

When a stalker gets too close to plus-size model Mae Cooper, it's time to hire some muscle.

Enter former military man turned executive protection officer Ziggy Thayer. Having spent years guarding billionaires, royalty, and rock 'n' roll greats, he's seen it all. From lavish parties through to every kind of excess.

There's no reason some Instagram stylista should throw him off his game. Even if she does have the most dangerous curves he's ever seen...

\* \* \* \*

### Strong: A Stage Dive Novella

When the girl of your dreams is kind of a nightmare.

As head of security to Stage Dive, one of the biggest rock bands in the world, Sam Knowles has plenty of experience dealing with trouble. But spoilt brat Martha Nicholson just might be the worst thing he's ever encountered. The beautiful troublemaker claims to have reformed, but Sam knows better than to think with what's in his pants. Unfortunately, it's not so easy to make his heart fall into line.

Martha's had her sights on the seriously built bodyguard for years. Quiet and conservative, he's not even remotely her type. So why the hell can't she get him out of her mind? There's more to her than the Louboutin wearing party-girl of previous years, however. Maybe it's time to let him in on that fact and deal with this thing between them.

# About Kylie Scott

Kylie is a *New York Times*, *Wall Street Journal*, and *USA Today* best-selling, Audie Award winning author. She has sold over 2,000,000 books and was voted Australian Romance Writer of the year, 2013, 2014, 2018, & 2019, by the Australian Romance Reader's Association. Her books have been translated into fourteen different languages.

# Discover 1001 Dark Nights

BAYOU by Heather Graham ~ SEARCHING FOR MINE by Jennifer Probst ~ DANCE OF DESIRE by Christopher Rice ~ ROUGH RHYTHM by Tessa Bailey ~ DEVOTED by Lexi Blake ~ Z by Larissa Ione ~ FALLING UNDER YOU by Laurelin Paige ~ EASY FOR KEEPS by Kristen Proby ~ UNCHAINED by Elisabeth Naughton ~ HARD TO SERVE by Laura Kaye ~ DRAGON FEVER by Donna Grant ~ KAYDEN/SIMON by Alexandra Ivy/Laura Wright ~ STRUNG UP by Lorelei James ~ MIDNIGHT UNTAMED by Lara Adrian ~ TRICKED by Rebecca Zanetti ~ DIRTY WICKED by Shayla Black ~ THE ONLY ONE by Lauren Blakely ~ SWEET SURRENDER by Liliana Hart

COLLECTION FOUR
ROCK CHICK REAWAKENING by Kristen Ashley ~ ADORING INK by Carrie Ann Ryan ~ SWEET RIVALRY by K. Bromberg ~ SHADE'S LADY by Joanna Wylde ~ RAZR by Larissa Ione ~ ARRANGED by Lexi Blake ~ TANGLED by Rebecca Zanetti ~ HOLD ME by J. Kenner ~ SOMEHOW, SOME WAY by Jennifer Probst ~ TOO CLOSE TO CALL by Tessa Bailey ~ HUNTED by Elisabeth Naughton ~ EYES ON YOU by Laura Kaye ~ BLADE by Alexandra Ivy/Laura Wright ~ DRAGON BURN by Donna Grant ~ TRIPPED OUT by Lorelei James ~ STUD FINDER by Lauren Blakely ~ MIDNIGHT UNLEASHED by Lara Adrian ~ HALLOW BE THE HAUNT by Heather Graham ~ DIRTY FILTHY FIX by Laurelin Paige ~ THE BED MATE by Kendall Ryan ~ NIGHT GAMES by CD Reiss ~ NO RESERVATIONS by Kristen Proby ~ DAWN OF SURRENDER by Liliana Hart

COLLECTION FIVE
BLAZE ERUPTING by Rebecca Zanetti ~ ROUGH RIDE by Kristen Ashley ~ HAWKYN by Larissa Ione ~ RIDE DIRTY by Laura Kaye ~ ROME'S CHANCE by Joanna Wylde ~ THE

MARRIAGE ARRANGEMENT by Jennifer Probst ~ SURRENDER by Elisabeth Naughton ~ INKED NIGHTS by Carrie Ann Ryan ~ ENVY by Rachel Van Dyken ~ PROTECTED by Lexi Blake ~ THE PRINCE by Jennifer L. Armentrout ~ PLEASE ME by J. Kenner ~ WOUND TIGHT by Lorelei James ~ STRONG by Kylie Scott ~ DRAGON NIGHT by Donna Grant ~ TEMPTING BROOKE by Kristen Proby ~ HAUNTED BE THE HOLIDAYS by Heather Graham ~ CONTROL by K. Bromberg ~ HUNKY HEARTBREAKER by Kendall Ryan ~ THE DARKEST CAPTIVE by Gena Showalter

COLLECTION SIX
DRAGON CLAIMED by Donna Grant ~ ASHES TO INK by Carrie Ann Ryan ~ ENSNARED by Elisabeth Naughton ~ EVERMORE by Corinne Michaels ~ VENGEANCE by Rebecca Zanetti ~ ELI'S TRIUMPH by Joanna Wylde ~ CIPHER by Larissa Ione ~ RESCUING MACIE by Susan Stoker ~ ENCHANTED by Lexi Blake ~ TAKE THE BRIDE by Carly Phillips ~ INDULGE ME by J. Kenner ~ THE KING by Jennifer L. Armentrout ~ QUIET MAN by Kristen Ashley ~ ABANDON by Rachel Van Dyken ~ THE OPEN DOOR by Laurelin Paige~ CLOSER by Kylie Scott ~ SOMETHING JUST LIKE THIS by Jennifer Probst ~ BLOOD NIGHT by Heather Graham ~ TWIST OF FATE by Jill Shalvis ~ MORE THAN PLEASURE YOU by Shayla Black ~ WONDER WITH ME by Kristen Proby ~ THE DARKEST ASSASSIN by Gena Showalter

COLLECTION SEVEN
THE BISHOP by Skye Warren ~ TAKEN WITH YOU by Carrie Ann Ryan ~ DRAGON LOST by Donna Grant ~ SEXY LOVE by Carly Phillips ~ PROVOKE by Rachel Van Dyken ~ RAFE by Sawyer Bennett ~ THE NAUGHTY PRINCESS by

TEASE ME by J. Kenner ~ FROM BLOOD AND ASH by
Jennifer L. Armentrout ~ QUEEN MOVE by Kennedy Ryan ~
THE HOUSE OF LONG AGO by Steve Berry and M.J. Rose ~
THE BUTTERFLY ROOM by Lucinda Riley ~ A KINGDOM
OF FLESH AND FIRE by Jennifer L. Armentrout ~ THE LAST
TIARA by M.J. Rose ~ THE CROWN OF GILDED BONES by
Jennifer L. Armentrout ~ THE MISSING SISTER by Lucinda
Riley ~ THE END OF FOREVER by Steve Berry and M.J. Rose
~ THE STEAL by C. W. Gortner and M.J. Rose ~ CHASING
SERENITY by Kristen Ashley ~ A SHADOW IN THE EMBER
by Jennifer L. Armentrout

## On Behalf of 1001 Dark Nights,

Liz Berry, M.J. Rose, and Jillian Stein would like to thank ~

Steve Berry
Doug Scofield
Benjamin Stein
Kim Guidroz
Social Butterfly PR
Asha Hossain
Chris Graham
Chelle Olson
Kasi Alexander
Jessica Saunders
Dylan Stockton
Kate Boggs
Richard Blake
and Simon Lipskar

Made in United States
North Haven, CT
02 November 2022

26191320R00061